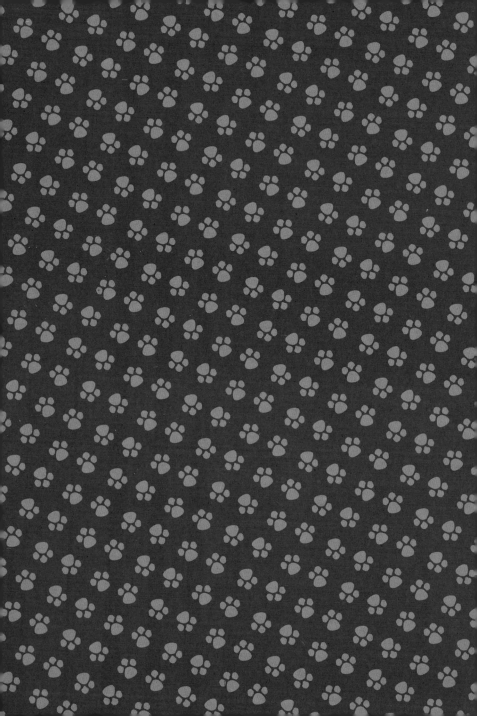

HELPER HOUNDS

King Tut

Helps Ming Stay Weird

Dedication
To my son Henrik,
Who shares my love of animal rescue,
Who live-texted me during his high-school
lock-down drill so I'd know the, well, drill,
And who asked the question long ago
that inspired this story.
Thanks. I love you.

HELPER HOUNDS
King Tut

Helps Ming Stay Weird

Caryn Rivadeneira
Illustrated by Priscilla Alpaugh

RED CHAIR
· PRESS ·

Egremont, Massachusetts

RED CHAIR PRESS
BOOKS FOR YOUNG READERS

www.redchairpress.com

 Free educator's guide at www.redchairpress.com/free-resources

Publisher's Cataloging-In-Publication Data

Names: Rivadeneira, Caryn Dahlstrand, author. | Alpaugh, Priscilla, illustrator.

Title: King Tut helps Ming stay weird / Caryn Rivadeneira ; illustrated by Priscilla Alpaugh.

Description: Egremont, Massachusetts : Red Chair Press, [2020] | Series: Helper hounds ; [book 5] | Interest age level: 006-009. | Includes facts about mutts. | Summary: "Ming often gets teased for being "weird." His curious mind and wild imagination make him extra nervous for his school's upcoming lockdown drill after a deadly dance hall shooting. His teacher calls the Helper Hounds to help calm his nerves-and King Tut comes to the rescue! King Tut knows all about being weird. After all, she is a female mutt with the name of a boy king! She's also been in some scary situations herself after being abandoned under a bridge as a puppy. King Tut helps Ming and his classmates through the lockdown drill. But will her tricks be enough when there's a real lockdown? Discover how King Tut helps Ming and his friends see the beauty in being "weird?""-- Provided by publisher.

Identifiers: ISBN 9781634409162 (hc) | ISBN 9781634409193 (sc) | ISBN 9781634409223 (ebook)

Subjects: : LCSH: Mixed breed dogs--Juvenile fiction. | Schools--Safety measures--Juvenile fiction. | Anxiety--Juvenile fiction. | Difference (Psychology)--Juvenile fiction. | CYAC: Mixed breed dogs--Fiction. | Schools--Safety measures--Fiction. | Anxiety--Fiction. | Difference (Psychology)--Fiction.

Classification: LCC PZ7.1.R57627 Ki 2021 (print) | LCC PZ7.1.R57627 (ebook) | DDC [E]--dc23

Library of Congress Control Number: 2020937699

Photos: iStock

Printed in the United States of America

0920 1P CGS21

CHAPTER 1

All around us, people cheered.

Above us, flags swayed, and the bright sun streamed through the skylights. It felt like we were in a parade. But we weren't. We were just walking—well, trotting really—through the airport terminal. The same as we do every time we get back from a Helper Hounds trip.

But this time, things felt different. The mood of the crowd was different. People were always happy to see us—in our bright red Helper Hounds vests—trotting in single file. But today's cheers were a mix of happiness and sadness. Which made sense. Most of the work the

Helper Hounds do is a mix of happiness and sadness too.

The cheers had started when a man ran past us. He was late for his flight. But when he caught a glimpse of Sparky's bouncing fur, swishing tail, and Helper Hounds vest, the man stopped, nodded, and began to clap.

The cheers grew louder as Robot, Penny, Noodle, Oscar, and I followed Sparky's lead into the bright terminal hallway. The crowd split to make room for us. People wiped tears and said, "Thank you, Helper Hounds!" or they whistled.

A few little kids and their parents asked if they could pet us.

So we stopped for a moment and let ourselves get a good petting. Eloise knelt down and picked me up. I am the littlest Helper Hound. It's easy for me to get lost in the mix— even though I am the weirdest looking. At least, that's what everyone tells me.

Anyway, while I was getting a terrific ear scratch from a tiny boy with a huge backpack, Mr. Tuttle, the leader of the Helper Hounds, said we needed to go.

"The Helper Hounds need to find the potty!" he said. Everyone laughed and moved back to let us through. But as we started our march through the terminal, another woman walked up.

"I know you have to go," the woman said. "But my brother was there... He was at the dance hall. He told me you visited..."

The woman wiped her eyes. Robot leaned against her legs. Sparky smiled up at her face— and wagged his tail in our faces.

"I haven't been able to get down to visit him until now," she said. "Thank you for being there."

Mr. Tuttle told her we were happy to go. And we were!

As soon as our Helper Humans heard about the terrible shooting at the dance hall, we knew we could help. The Helper Hounds couldn't save the lives of people who had died, but we could help the people who lived.

And so, we spent our time doing what we do best: sitting, listening, and snuggling. Some days, we visited hospitals and heard stories of what happened. We lay on hospital beds and snuggled as people cried or vented their fear or pain. Other days, we visited the dance hall and sat with families who had lost loved ones. We stood with people who held candles and led prayers. We marched with people sad and angry about gun violence. We visited schools to hang out with kids who felt afraid and helped them talk about it.

Eloise, my person—or Helper Human— reached out to touch the woman's arm.

"Is your brother okay?" Eloise said.

"He lost a good friend," she said. "And he's shaken up. But the visit from the dogs made his day. He hasn't talked much about what happened, but he told me all about the visit. Is one of you King Tut?"

My tail wagged at the sound of my name.

"*This* is King Tut," Eloise said.

The woman scratched my head and smiled.

"You look more like a Muppet than King Tut," she said. "My brother never liked dogs much. More of a cat guy. But I can see why he liked you. You're a silly little thing."

"She is," Eloise said. I licked the woman's hand.

"*She?*" the woman said. "The girl who would be king. The dogs who would be heroes. What a world…"

The woman took a selfie with us and then rushed off to her flight.

Penny's Helper Human, Miguel, spied the "Pet Relief Room" down the terminal and suggested we head off. You might think it was weird to be cheered on in the relief room. But it turned out to be kind of fun. It wasn't even scary. It reminded me of my potty-training days.

The cheering continued for us all the way

to baggage claim. Apparently, news of our visit to the Dance Hall Shooting families made the news all over the world. And since this was an international airport, people from all over the world were there to cheer us.

By the time we had our bags and got loaded into the Helper Hounds van, we were pooped. All us dogs curled up on our seats and took good long snoozes.

But while we slept, our Helper Humans' phones buzzed. News coverage of our visits always meant calls, emails, and texts. Lots of people needed help!

Eloise scratched my back as I twitched and bar-bar-barked in my sleep.

"At least our next case is close by," she said. "Right at our school! Looks like Ming in Ms. Hanson's class needs some company. He's been reading about the shooting and about our lockdown drill coming up. He's really nervous.

You're good at getting through things that make you nervous, right Tut?"

Eloise likes to ask me questions while I'm dreaming away (this time about hopping after bunnies in a meadow). That's okay. I'm always listening for her.

I opened one eye and rested my head on her hand.

"I'll take that as a yes," Eloise said.

CHAPTER 2

Eloise dropped our bags in the hallway. As she unclipped my leash and Helper Hounds vest, she said, "Just need to ask Ming's mom what is up—and then time for a nap for me!"

I barked my support of naps and headed to my bowl for a slurp of water. Eloise rushed to grab it out from under me. She thought I needed "fresh" water. But I tell you: I like water better when it's been sitting around a while. It begins to taste like the room smells. And I like that!

But I happily licked up the fresh, cool water Eloise set back down in front of me. Then I gobbled the kibble she shook into my food bowl.

Eloise sat at her desk in the kitchen and typed into her computer. She told Ming's mom I could help Ming.

"The other kids tease Ming so much for being *weird*," Eloise turned to tell me. "Breaks my heart how mean they can be. He *is* curious about 'weird' things."

Eloise shook her head. She looked at the curio cabinet full of strange family treasures.

"Someday people will see that as a good thing," she said. "But right now his curious mind makes kids tease him—and it makes him nervous. We can help."

I barked and stuck my face in the bowl for two more slurps of water. When I lifted my head, water dripped from my beard.

Eloise scratched my head. "Good night, King Tut, you weird, weird dog," she said and snuck off to her bedroom. I jumped onto my favorite chair—just in front of the wide windows that overlooked the backyard. From here, I could keep an eye on the bunnies, squirrels, red robins, and black crows that visited. Sometimes I barked at them. Other times, I just kept my eyes on their movements. Wildlife guests were welcome *in* my backyard, but I didn't want them going near my collection of half-inflated soccer balls I kept around the yard.

But the animals kept to themselves, so I let my eyes grow heavy and sunk deeper into the chair cushion.

I couldn't help but think back to how far I'd come. After all, it wasn't so long ago that I was just a tiny puppy shivering under a bridge. Back then, I hid when squirrels or mice or centipedes crawled past my bed of dried leaves, newspaper, and empty bread bags. Back then, I wondered if I'd ever be warm or full or dry or loved.

Everything changed when Eloise heard my cries.

CHAPTER 3

I don't remember *how* I ended up under that bridge. I just remember waking up and *being* there. Weird feeling. Actually, *scary* feeling is more like it.

I was tiny then. I was all alone. I was hungry. I was cold. I was scared. I had no idea how to do anything without my mom or brothers and sisters.

But as scary as it was, under a bridge isn't the worst place in the world for a young pup. There's lots to listen to and lots to explore.

Above the bridge, cars and bikes rumbled by—day and night. Under the bridge, a small creek worked its way through some woods. The creek was pretty terrific. The creek meant I had plenty to drink—and lots of animals to watch.

Ducks drifted through the creek. Sometimes a beaver gnawed down sticks to build its dam. Slick otters dove in and out of the water. Foxes trotted along the banks. Squirrels dashed and bunnies hopped around. And birds—sparrows, robins, crows, and falcons—flew everywhere.

I stayed tucked tight in my pile of leaves and bread bags and watched and watched. Most days, I was too nervous to venture out. But sometimes, I'd smell something that seemed like it would fill my rumbling tummy, so I'd sneak out of my pile and shake off. Then I'd sniff around carefully for the bit of bread or French fries that made their way under the bridge.

When the coast was clear of animals, I'd head to the creek bed and stick my snout in the cool water. At first, I'd pull my paws back fast when they hit the water. But then, I learned to like the way the water felt on the pads of my feet. I'd stomp my feet in water and bite at the splashes all around me. It was fun. Well, it was fun until my splashing got out of hand, and I fell in. That got scary. I wasn't good at swimming back then (I am now). So when my head popped up, I wasn't sure what to do. But my legs paddled and paddled until I climbed back out of the creek.

I shook myself off on the edge of the creek. Two ducks quacked behind me. I jumped. I hoped they didn't see me, but I got the feeling they were laughing. Anyway, that day things started to feel a little lonelier. The weather was getting cooler. My tummy felt emptier than ever. I cried a lot then. And barked. But no matter how many cars or bikes rumbled above the bridge, no one heard me.

When thunderstorms blew by, the sounds got scarier. Loud cracks and booms rang in the sky. Leaves and branches hissed in the wind. Sometimes the squirrels and bunnies would join me under the bridge. We would all claim our space and shake in our spots. I would bark and howl and hope that would scare the thunder as much as the thunder scared me.

Sometimes that worked. The thunder ran away! It grew softer and softer each time. But other times, it didn't. So after a while, I'd just curl up like every other night and fall asleep to the sounds of the creek and the cars and the thunder and my own cries.

But then one morning, Eloise heard me. Eloise was at the creek taking pictures for her classroom. I was curled up—and already crying. That morning was cold. I was hungry and feeling too tired to hunt around for scraps of bread. So I just cried and cried and barked my best puppy barks.

"Hello?" Eloise said. Then she clicked her tongue. "Is there a puppy in there?"

Eloise knelt under the bridge.

I shook myself out of my pile and Eloise laughed.

"My goodness," she said. "How on earth did you get here?"

Then she reached over and picked me up. Eloise held me to her face and said, "I'm Eloise Jones. Who are you? Are you even a puppy or a bunny? You are tiny. And you must be so hungry."

Eloise held me close to her chest and reached into a bag. She broke off a piece of graham cracker.

"Not exactly the best puppy food," she said as she held the cracker in front of my tiny snout.

I didn't know what she was talking about. It was the best food I had ever had! I munched it down and sniffed her hand for more.

Eloise giggled and broke off two more bits. I gobbled them up.

"You eat nicely for a starving pup," she said. "Not biting me at all. Good soft mouth. I like that."

Once again, I had no idea what she was talking about. But every time I took a cracker nicely, Eloise told me I was a good puppy and gave me another cracker. I liked that. I could keep this up all day.

Eloise pulled me close to her face and looked me all over.

"You can't be more than two months old, little...uh...lady?" She said. "However did you get here?"

I wished I could tell her. But as I said: I don't remember how I got there. I have faint memories of my mom and siblings. If I think real hard, I remember smelling cardboard and pee. But the rest is a blur.

Maybe it's for the best I can't remember. Eloise mumbled something about the "monsters" that would leave a tiny, helpless puppy like me here. If I used to live with monsters, I'm glad I forgot!

Eloise grabbed the sweatshirt from around her waist and tucked it around me.

"How about you come home with me?" She said.

Next thing I knew I was curled up on the seat of her car. It was warm and dry and smelled like heaven. And this was only the beginning.

CHAPTER 4

Eloise and I live in a big house. And when I say big, I mean: BIG! It's huge. And it's not just because I'm small.

Our house has three floors (not including the old creepy cellar). Each floor has so many rooms, you can wander through doors, down hallways, poke your nose into hallways and closets and nooks all day, and never get bored. I know this from experience!

The very first day Eloise brought me home, I wandered and sniffed and wandered and sniffed. All day. I only got stuck once and lost twice. Good thing Eloise followed me everywhere that day. I only had to bark and whine for help and—*voila!*—Eloise was right there to help. It was only my first day with Eloise and already she heard my cry and picked me up—four times! That's the best feeling.

Anyway, lots of people asked Eloise how a teacher could afford such a huge house. Eloise told me she wished she had the guts to tell people it was none of their business. But, Eloise was way too nice to say something so rude. Besides, the story of how she got the house was really interesting and fun to tell!

So Eloise would tell them the weird truth: Her grandparents were inventors. For almost forty years they tinkered in the basement of the farmhouse they lived in back then. They invented all kinds of weird farm things: pig blankets, mouse houses, cat carts, and horse skirts.

But it turned out that people didn't want to

have to wash their pigs' blankets. People didn't want mice in *any* kind of house. Cats didn't want to pull carts and horses didn't want to wear skirts.

People laughed at her grandparents. All around town, people would roll their eyes and talk about the weird old couple who made bat hats and cow ribbons.

But her grandparents never gave up. They had fun inventing weird things—and knew one day people would understand.

Then one day, Eloise's grandmother said: "What if dogs wore vests?"

Eloise's grandfather asked why a dog would wear a vest.

"Well, if the dog were working," she said. "Like when Tumbler goes into the field with us. It would be handy if he could carry some of the tools."

Eloise's grandfather nodded and they got to work.

Turns out, people *wanted* their dogs to wear vests—and dogs didn't mind at all.

Farmers all around put in orders for the dog vests. Everyone loved them. Magazines ran stories about this amazing and handy new invention.

And then people from cities and towns all over began to call. Could they make vests for dogs that worked in places besides farms?

They could! And soon, farm dogs, ranch dogs, police dogs, rescue dogs, airport-sniffer dogs, and seeing-eye dogs all across the country wore vests made by the Hund Vest company— owned by Eloise's grandparents.

Her grandparents made a lot of money. They built a big house, right in town. Right next to some of the people who used to laugh at them.

The house had three floors—not including the creepy cellar. Each floor had so many rooms—oh, right—I already told you about this.

They built the house we live in!

Anyway, long story short: The business grew and grew. Eloise's mom ran the company. They kept making vests but also made leashes and collars and toys. When Eloise's mom came back from a trip to Egypt with plans to make Egyptian-print collars, like the ancient pharaohs used for their dogs, the country went nuts. The King Tut display was touring the country, and everyone wanted dog collars fashioned with scarab beetles and pyramids like the pharaoh dogs used to wear.

Eloise was proud of what her family did—but Eloise didn't want to work for the company. She wanted to teach kids how to paint and take pictures and to understand how important art and creativity and *weirdness* really are.

So Eloise became a teacher—and let her brother and sister take over the company. But Eloise got to take over the big house. Her siblings thought it was too old and weird. But Eloise loved it because she felt her grandparents' creative spirits running through every room. Eloise put the "failed" inventions on display. Sometimes she brought them into school.

"Maybe no one wanted a pig blanket or a horse skirt, but my grandparents never gave

up," Eloise would tell her students. "They let their creativity run wild—and never stopped dreaming or imagining and working hard. Even when they failed, they succeeded because they kept at it."

"People thought my grandparents were so weird," Eloise would say. "They got made fun of all the time. People thought they were too different and too crazy! And they *were* weird and they *were* different. But that's what made them amazing people. I'm so proud of them. And I'd be proud of them whether they became successes or not."

It was a good speech. And Eloise believed it. In fact, because Eloise believed that creativity and hard work could make any dream come true, Eloise began to dream with me.

On the second day I was at her house, Eloise wondered what my name should be.

"You look like a mutt," she said. "But you act

like a king. And I found you on the banks of a river. Just like Moses. But that's not quite right…"

Eloise looked up at the curio cabinet next to us. In it was the picture of a dog collar her mother had brought back from Egypt. She smiled.

"What about: King Tut the Mutt?" She asked me.

What could I say? I barked!

"But if you're going to be a king with humble, riverside roots and that weird hairdo, you better be ready to do great things in this world," Eloise said.

I was ready. I just didn't know what for!

CHAPTER 5

The big things started just a few weeks later.

"I just got off the phone with my principal," Eloise said. She picked me up and held me in front of her face. I got a little bigger over that first summer at my new house, but not much. "Guess what he said."

I had no idea so I just licked Eloise on the nose.

She laughed, scratched my head, and pulled me close.

"You, King Tut the Mutt, get to come to school with me this fall," she said. "Maybe not every day. But Principal Jackson agreed it would be good for the students to see how a puppy grows and gets trained. I just have to find a way to tie it into my art lessons, which might be hard…"

Eloise stared out the window as she always does when she's dreaming or imagining.

"Got it," Eloise said. "If I can train you to sit *still*, we can work on painting you."

So two weeks before school started, Eloise started *my* lessons. Every day we'd work on learning to sit, lie down, stay, heel, roll over, speak… It was really fun. I loved learning and was good at all the tricks.

For the first day of school, Eloise asked her brother if the Hund Vest company could make me a special vest for school. Eloise sent over designs. A week later, she opened a package.

"King Tut!" She called. I was two floors up nosing through a back storage closet, but I heard her clearly. I skidded through the hallways and down the stairs.

Eloise stood in the front hallway—a tiny gold vest in her hands.

"Let's see how it fits," she said. I lifted my front two paws so she could slip my little legs into the openings and then sucked in my bitty belly while she Velcro-ed the strap. Then I shook. It stayed on.

"It's perfect," Eloise said. "Fit for a King Tut."

I must admit: the gold fabric went really well with my white fluffs. Black scarabs dotted the vest. The words *King Tut the Mutt, School Dog* ran across the back.

"Scarabs symbolize rebirth or resurrection," Eloise told me. "And you had a sort of rebirth— from scrappy dog under that bridge to a King going to school."

And she was right.

• • •

I loved school right away. And the kids loved me.

I slept in a cozy kennel next to Eloise's desk for a chunk of the day. But at certain times, Eloise would call me out. The kids would play with me, help train me, or sit and draw me. When they'd paint or draw me, I would stay still like a statue. When they trained me, I helped them learn how to reward me with treats (the best part). And when we'd play, I'd run or tug or fetch.

Whatever I did, I tried to make them laugh. My ears would flop and bounce, or I'd tumble and roll. The kids would laugh till their faces turned red. I loved that.

But one boy never laughed. One boy never played with or trained me. Ming would draw me (really well in fact!). But he'd add strange features to my pictures: a unicorn's horn, a rainbow tail, or he'd set me on top of a pyramid's point.

"That's a *weird* picture," Eva would say with a smack of her tongue. Ming would sigh and hang his head.

When other kids gathered round, Ming stayed in his seat and watched. His eyebrows would scrunch, and he would scribble or draw on his sketchpad.

Then Ming did something the other kids never did. Ming would suggest something for me to do.

"King Tut would be a good fire dog," Ming would say. "She could stay low—away from the smoke."

The other kids would disagree—except Luis.

"Yeah, she might be good at that, Ming!" Luis would say.

"No, she wouldn't," Tina said. "King Tut is too fluffy. Her hair would catch fire."

"King Tut would be good on a fishing boat," Ming would say. "She's so small. She'd stay out of the way."

"No she wouldn't," Paul said. "King Tut would try to play with the fish when they flopped around."

"King Tut would be good in the White House," Ming said. "She could sleep on a sofa and help the President relax."

"No, she wouldn't," Mallory said. "The President is too busy. She'd never get to play. She needs to play."

And on and on it went. The students rolled
their eyes at Ming. All the time.

And they got so used to him not coming
over to play or being too weird when he did,
that they stopped inviting him over. But I never
stopped *going* over by Ming. I knew he was
different. I could feel he was lonely. And he
knew he was weird. But I liked him for all those
reasons. So when Eloise had the kids settled

on the floor sketching or hearing about an art project, I'd sneak over by Ming and snooze beneath his desk.

Ming would lean down to pet me and then get back to work.

One day, Ming suggested that I would make a good sheep-herder.

Eva huffed loudly.

"She would *not* make a good sheep dog," she said. "The sheep would *trample* her. You are so weird, Ming."

"Eva!" Eloise said. "That was very rude. Apologize to Ming."

Eva said sorry. Ming looked down at his sketchpad as the kids laughed. I ran over to Ming and jumped up so my paws landed on his lap.

Ming smiled and reached down to pet me.

I took two steps back. He smiled and reached his hand forward.

Ming stood up and stepped toward me. I took two more steps back. Ming smiled again and walked forward.

Soon, Ming was up front with the rest of the kids. I sat. Ming sat criss-cross applesauce. I climbed into his lap.

"Looks like Ming was right," Luis said. "King Tut herded him over here."

Eloise nodded and thanked Luis for that "observation."

But Ming wasn't done with the suggestions.

"King Tut would make a good Helper Hound," Ming said. "I read about them online. King Tut helps me, and she could help other people too."

This time, no one laughed.

Luis was the first to yell, "YESSS!" But the rest of the class quickly joined in.

"But the Helper Hounds are much *bigger* than King Tut," Eva said.

"That is true," said Eloise.

"Every day you say it doesn't matter that I'm different—or even weird," Ming said. "I can do or be anything. I belong everywhere. That's the same for King Tut."

Eloise nodded.

That night Eloise called her sister. Hund Vests made the Helper Hounds vests. Eloise was sure her sister knew Mr. Tuttle, the founder of Helper Hounds.

Next thing I knew, I was off to Helper Hounds University with the big dogs.

Mr. Tuttle worried my small size would keep me from doing a good job. But I had survived living under a bridge. And now, I spent my days in a busy classroom. I knew being a Helper Hound would be no sweat.

CHAPTER 6

Long story short: I graduated from Helper Hounds University and became an official Helper Hound. Of course, I was the smallest Helper Hound. And, I sensed, the *weirdest* one. My hair was all scruff. My tail hung kind of wonky. And I was a girl dog named after a boy king. But that was okay. In fact, being a small, weird Helper Hound comes in very handy.

Although, I had to have my Helper Hounds vest *custom made*. Know what else comes in handy? When your human "aunt" and "uncle" own the vest company!

Eloise's sister dropped off my special vest.

All the Helper Hounds vests look identical. They are bright red with "Helper Hound" written across them. But my vest had a secret. Underneath, Eloise's sister sewed "King Tut the Mutt of Hund House."

Had I mentioned that was the name of our house? Well, it was. Eloise's grandparents named it Hund House after the company that made them enough money to build the house.

From the moment I put my vest on, Eloise and I started going on cases. We helped kids all across the state and country! Sometimes we got on planes. Sometimes we stayed overnight in hotels. Sometimes we just had to drive a couple hours.

This was the first time we got a request from our own school!

Turned out, Ming was worried about a "lockdown drill" coming up.

Who could blame him? Lots of kids get

nervous about these drills. It's scary to imagine what would happen if someone came into school with a gun or threatening words. But when Ming got worried, he had a hard time calming down. He had a hard time listening and doing what he needed to. The kids would say mean things and call him weird—even more than they normally did!

That's why his mom hoped I could help.

"I wish the world wasn't like this," Eloise said as she read the email from Ming's mom. "I wish we didn't need lockdown drills to practice hiding or fighting. And I wish we didn't make fun of people who aren't like us!"

Eloise pulled me up on her lap and looked right at me.

"Do you think you can help Ming not feel so afraid? Can you help him relax as he goes through the drill?"

Eloise asked me this. But we both knew the

answer. I could help Ming—for sure!

"And here's the harder question," Eloise said. "Can we help Ming learn that being different is good? That there's a place for everyone?"

Eloise looked at my scruff and my wonky tail and smiled at me. "Actually," she said. "You probably already proved that!"

The next day, Eloise met with Ming's homeroom teacher and the principal. I came too. They agreed that on Tuesday—the day of the drill—I would hang out in Ming's classroom all day. Ming's teacher, Ms. Hanson, would keep the kennel by her desk. But I could sit by Ming whenever Ming wanted.

It was going to be a great day!

Happily, Tuesday came fast. Just after the bell rang and after the students listened to announcements and said the pledge, Eloise knocked on Ms. Hanson's door.

"Special delivery," Eloise said.

Eloise made the "speak" command with her hand. So I barked. The kids cheered.

"King Tut is going to hang out with us today," Ms. Hanson said. "Ming thought she could help us get ready for our lockdown drill."

"How will she help?" Eva asked. "What if she barks while we're hiding?"

"Great questions," Eloise said. Eloise pointed to my vest. "She's got her Helper Hounds vest on today. King Tut is smart. She knows when she's working as a Helper Hound and when she's just hanging out at school. She barks much less in her Helper Hounds vest. Plus, we can tell King Tut when to bark."

Eloise did the "speak" command. I barked.

"And," Eloise said. "I can tell her to shush. I want to teach you all how to do that too."

Eloise and I went to the front of the classroom. Eloise called Ming up.

"Ming," Eloise said. "Do you remember

how to tell King Tut to bark?"

Ming motioned the command with his hand.
I barked.

"Now, try this." Eloise brought her finger to
her mouth. "You can shush King Tut just like
you shush a person. I'll get her to bark and then
you try."

Eloise made the bark-bark-bark motion. This
meant for me to bark my head off. So I did. But
then Ming stepped forward. He put
his finger to his lips.

I stopped.

The kids cheered again.
I wagged my tail.

"But more than that,"
Eloise said. "King Tut
can help everyone
stay calm. That's
one of the most
important things!"

"I don't know," said Eva. "This sounds like another one of Ming's weird ideas…"

"It doesn't sound weird to me," said Luis. "When it storms at home, I feel better when my dog, Petey, is up on my bed."

Ming smiled at Luis. Luis reached out a hand. They bumped fists.

"All right then," said Ms. Hanson. "Time to get back to *actual* class. Ming, can you please be in charge of King Tut?"

Ming nodded and called me over to his desk. He gave me the down command Eloise showed him before she left. Then he handed me my bone. I chewed away on that while Ms. Hanson began her lesson.

Every once in a while, I felt Ming's hand on my back. At first, his fingers shook as he scratched me. But then he would settle down. And so did I. I fell into a nice, deep sleep.

CHAPTER 7

Who knows how long I would've kept on sleeping. I imagine all day. But somewhere in the middle of me dreaming about swimming with otters down by my old creek, the bell sounded. Principal Jackson came over the loud speaker:

"Attention students: This is a lockdown drill. I repeat: This is a lockdown drill."

The classroom door snapped shut and clicked.

"Okay, students," Ms. Hanson said. "Just as we talked about. Everyone in the corner please. And stay very still and quiet."

I stood up—as did most of the students.

But Ming stayed frozen in his seat. As kids shuffled toward the corner furthest from the door, I bumped my nose into Ming's leg.

Ming still didn't move. Well, except that his leg bounced beneath the desk.

"Ming, please," Ms. Hanson said. "To the corner. You can walk with King Tut."

"But I was thinking," Ming said. "If there were a shooter, wouldn't the shooter know we hide in the corner? I mean. If the shooter was ever a student?"

Ms. Hanson sighed.

"Perhaps," she said. "But this is the drill. This is what Officer Landry came in and talked to us about. This is how the police say we stay safest."

"Stop being so weird, Ming! Let's go!" Eva whispered loudly.

"Stop being so mean, Eva," Luis said. "Don't worry, Ming. You can do it."

Ming nodded. He took a deep breath. Ming reached his hand toward my vest and read: "Helper Hound."

"You need to help me," Ming whispered. "I'm scared."

I nudged Ming again with my nose. Then I took two steps back—just like we did in art

class. Ming smiled and slid down his chair. I scooted back more. Ming stood up. I scooted two more steps. Ming took two steps. Then I stopped. I moved toward Ming. He bent down to pick me up. Ming scratched my neck as he walked step-by-step toward the corner.

When we reached the other students, Luis patted Ming on the back.

"Good job," Luis said.

"King Tut helped me," Ming said.

"She's a good girl," Luis said.

Ming nodded.

Ms. Hanson shushed everyone.

"This may just be a drill, but we need to be quiet," she said.

Ming put his finger to his lips and gave me the "shush" sign. I relaxed in his arms and kept my snout shut.

The cluster of children in the corner began to feel tight. They squirmed and coughed as the minutes ticked on. Even I had trouble staying still. Ming's breathing had settled. I knew he was relaxed. So I wiggled in Ming's arms until he put me down. I liked to snuggle. But like the kids, it was best for me to stand during the drill. As a Helper Hound, it was important that I be prepared.

Finally, the bell boop-booped again. Principal Jackson came over the intercom. Everyone relaxed and moved a step away from each other.

"Our lockdown drill has ended," she said. "Thank you, everyone, for behaving so well. If anyone would like to talk about today's drill, counselors are available. Just tell your teacher. Also, King Tut the Helper Hound is on hand."

Eva snickered.

"Pretty sure only Ming needs King Tut…"

"Eva!" Ms. Hanson said. "Your stress is coming out in terrible ways. We can talk about it over lunch recess today."

Eva kicked her shoe into the ground.

Luis bent down to pet me before Ming walked me over to Ms. Hanson's desk.

"She can sleep in her kennel if she needs to," Ming said. "I feel okay now."

"You did well, Ming," Ms. Hanson said. "I'm proud of you." Ms. Hanson smiled down at me. "Proud of *both* of you."

For whatever reason, that night I did not sleep well. I was used to exciting events as a Helper Hound. But after today's drill, something didn't sit right with me. Maybe it was a smell in the wind. Maybe it was an energy I picked up in the classroom. Either way, I knew tomorrow would be another big day. And I knew I needed to be back in Ms. Hanson's classroom. How was I going to make that happen?

CHAPTER 8

The next morning at school, I made a huge fuss. I didn't settle into my crate like I normally do when Eloise gets her supplies ready for the day. I didn't sniff around the room like I do when I'm bored.

Instead, I followed Eloise and whined.

I had to find a way to tell Eloise I needed to be back with Ms. Hanson's class.

Eloise brought her finger to her mouth. I stopped whining.

Then I thought of another idea. My Helper Hounds vest was still at school. Eloise had it in my bag under her desk. So I ran over and pulled my vest out. I sat in front of it and wagged and wagged my tail until Eloise picked me up.

"Silly girl," Eloise said. "What on earth has gotten into you?"

Eloise put me down and picked up the Helper Hounds vest. She took two steps toward her desk and then stopped.

"Wait," she said. "You want to wear this?"

She held my vest toward me. I barked and wiggled and shook.

"What's going on?" Eloise asked.

I had no way of telling her, of course. But as she snapped the vest on my body, I relaxed. When she was done, I trotted toward the door and scratched at it.

"Where do we need to go?" Eloise asked.

I galloped down the hallway and paused at Room 112.

"Ms. Hanson's room," Eloise said. "You want to be back with Ming? I think he's doing okay today."

But Eloise tapped on the door. Ms. Hanson opened it and smiled when she saw me.

"What a lovely surprise," Ms. Hanson said. The kids behind her waved and said hello.

"King Tut led me here this morning," Eloise said. "I'm not sure what to say, except that I think she wants to be here with you today."

"Fine with me," Ms. Hanson said. "Is it okay with you all?"

The class clapped and said, "Yes!"

Eloise walked me over to Ming. He reached down to pet me, and I licked his hand. I sat down next to Ming's desk but looked around for Eva. When I did sleep last night, I dreamt that Eva was being chased by rabbits. I chased the rabbits and scared them away, of course. But normally people weren't in my dreams about bunnies. That was weird.

Eloise walked back into the classroom with my crate. "Just in case she needs some alone time later," Eloise said.

"Or a time out," said Eva.

Eloise nodded. "King Tut should behave herself," Eloise said. "But you are right. Sometimes we all need a time out from our duties."

"Having to sit by Ming all day would make me want a time out," Eva said.

She whispered it. But I could hear her. So could Ming. His hand shook as he bent down to pet me.

"Why do you choose unkindness?" Ms. Hanson asked.

Eva shrugged. "Ming's weird. He's easy to

make fun of."

Eloise sighed. "One day you'll learn to appreciate the *'weird'* people," Eloise said. "They're the ones who change the world—and save lives."

"Whatever," Eva said.

"We'll talk again at lunch today," Ms. Hanson said. "And..."

But before Ms. Hanson could finish, the bell booped again. Principal Jackson spoke over the loudspeaker:

"Attention: Lockdown. Lockdown. This is not a drill."

The door slammed shut. The lock clicked into place.

"What's going on?" asked Luis.

"I don't know," Ms. Hanson said. "Come on."

The children rose from their seats and scrambled toward the corner. Everyone except Ming and Eva.

"Kids, let's go," Ms. Hanson said.

I sniffed the air. I could smell her fear across the room. I could practically taste the sniffles from the kids.

Ming breathed deep and bent down to pick me up.

"King, you helped me before," Ming said. "You can help me again."

Ming stood up and held me close. He started to walk toward the corner where the kids clung close together.

"Eva, please," Ms. Hanson said.

"I can't," Eva said. She began to sob. "I can't move. I'm too scared."

Ming stopped. He turned toward Eva and held me out to her. I paddled my paws in the air just like I was swimming to Eva.

"Take King Tut," Ming said. "She helps."

Eva nodded and reached for me. I licked her face and then jumped off her lap.

"Come here," Eva said. "Come here."

Normally I obey commands to "come," but getting Eva to move was more important. So I ignored her and took two steps back.

"Follow her," Ming said from the safety of the group. Luis patted Ming on the back.

Eva shook her head. "I can't."

"You can," Ming said. "You have to."

"But what if we get shot," Eva said.

"We'll be okay," Ming said. "I read a lot about lockdowns. Because I'm weird, you know?"

"You're not weird," Luis whispered.

"No, I am," Ming said. "But that's okay. Because that's how I know stuff. Just follow King Tut, Eva. You have to."

I wiggled my fanny and let out a low growl. When dogs growl, we're just warning people. Sometimes dogs growl to warn of a bite. Sometimes dogs growl to warn that we hear something. Sometimes we growl because something is about to happen.

Eva needed a warning. We had no time.

Eva scooted forward in her chair to reach me. I took two more steps back.

"Good job," Ming said. "If you're still scared take baby steps. You can even crawl!"

Eva nodded and slid onto the floor. She ran her hand across her nose. I jumped toward Eva, and together we moved along the floor to the rest of the group.

Ms. Hanson held her arms open for Eva. Eva fell into them and sobbed. Ms. Hanson rubbed her back and told her it would be okay.

I sat on the ground in front of Ming and Luis. I sniffed the air to smell what I could. No bomb smell. No gun smell. No danger at all.

But still, all around me, children shook and sniffled.

Ming bent down to pick me up. He shook harder than anyone.

CHAPTER 9

Boooooop. The time between the bell and Principal Jackson's voice felt like forever.

Everyone turned to look at the speaker on the wall behind us.

When she finally spoke, the children relaxed.

"The hard lockdown is over," she said. "You may move around the classroom and the school. Teachers, please check your emails for more information."

A few children cheered but most still looked worried.

Ms. Hanson turned to her computer.

"Everyone have a seat," Eloise said.

But no one moved. Everyone watched Ms. Hanson read.

"Okay," Ms. Hanson said. "Turns out, the bank on South Street got robbed. That's only three blocks away. The robbers had guns, and they ran toward our school."

Children gasped.

"That's when they locked us down," Ms. Hanson said. "They caught one of the robbers. And they know where the other two are. The police will have them soon."

"But are they still near the school?" Luis asked.

"Probably not," said Ming. Everyone turned to look at him. "I read a lot about criminals..." Ming paused and looked at Eva. "Aren't you going to say how weird I am?" Ming said.

Eva shook her head.

"No," she said. "Keep going."

Ming smiled and explained that the robbers

would have run in different directions. They would have a "meeting place." The robber they caught probably told the police where that was. No way it would be in the same direction anyone ran at first.

"Thank you, Ming," Ms. Hanson said. "I'm very proud of how well you all did. This was very scary. If anyone needs to talk to anyone, school counselors are available. Or talk to your parents or me... In fact, I'd like to hear how you're feeling."

"Happy it's over," Mallory said.

"Hoping they catch the other robbers," Paul said.

"Wondering if my mom knows," said Luis.

"Your parents and caregivers got an email and text alert," Ms. Hanson said. "So she knows."

Eva raised her hand.

"I keep thinking about Ms. Jones's grandparents," Eva said.

"You do?" Eloise said.

"Yeah," Eva said. "Like how you told us they were weird. They had all these weird ideas, and people thought they were strange. But then... they had the idea for vests for working dogs. And that helped people! And now, we have King Tut. She's weird. She's got a weird name, and she's not like the other Helper Hounds—she's so little and her tail is so long. But she helped me today.

"And then, we have Ming…"

The students around us held their breath. What was Eva going to say?

"Ming, sometimes you *are* weird," she said. "It's weird to me that you study old Egyptian beetles and read about criminals. But I'm really glad you're weird. You have good ideas, and you helped me."

Eva walked over to Ming and hugged him. Ming blushed and smiled.

"How about we all thank Ming and King Tut for their help today?" Ms. Hanson said.

"To two weirdos," said Ming. Then he picked me up and hugged me.

EPILOGUE

Dear King Tut,

Guess what! We had a fire drill today. And I was the leader out of the room. I wasn't scared at all. Eva wasn't scared either. At least, she wasn't scared of the fire. She did get scared when I picked up a cicada beetle to show her.

Cicadas are really pretty. They have purple heads and clear wings. Have you seen one? Some dogs eat them. I'm not sure if you should or not... Wait I just looked it up. They're okay for dogs to eat if you ever want to try one.

Anyway, when I showed Eva the beetle, she started screaming. That scared the cicada and it started flapping. Pretty soon all the kids were screaming and flapping, too.

I worried the cicada would get stepped on, but it was fine. Eva rescued it. She says she's not normally scared of bugs. She's only scared when someone pops them in front of her face. Ms. Hanson told me I should ask before I put a bug in someone's face.

What's new with you? Any fun cases?

I can't wait to see you when you come to the assembly next week. Eva and I are assembly buddies now. We're coloring a sign to hold up so you can see where we're sitting.

Love,

Ming

King Tut's
Tips on Including Everyone

It's easy to dismiss people—or dogs!—because we think they're different or maybe weird. Like how the people in town thought Eloise's grandparents were foolish. Or how Eva rolled her eyes at and teased Ming for his weird ideas and hobbies. Or how people don't expect me to be a Helper Hound because I'm little and shaggy and have a wonky tail. Plus, I'm a girl dog with a boy name. Some people think that's weird! But weird people—and dogs!—make the world a better place. Here's how you can appreciate and include weirdness:

TIP #1: Stop Assuming! To assume is to guess ahead of time how or what someone should be like or how they should act. Forget that! Instead, learn to look at others with fresh eyes.

Every person, dog, cat, pig, and turtle is different. Thank goodness!

TIP #2: Study Weird Things Most cool inventions or cures were made by people who got laughed at. Think about how weird everyone thought the inventors of Apple© were! They worked out of a garage for Pete's sake. When we know the history and the important role of "weird" or different people, we stop seeing people as weird!

TIP #3: Make Weird Friends It's always best to have a few friends who are different from us. And the best kind of people are willing to be silly and creative, different, and weird!

TIP #4: Let Your Weird Show The world needs us to be us—and let's face it: Most of us are a little weird and wonderful. So be it!

FUN FACTS

About Mutts

You probably know there are different breeds, or kinds, of dogs. But sometimes, a dog isn't just one breed. It can be a mix of two or more breeds. When an animal is a mixture of different kinds of dogs, we call it a mixed-breed, or a mutt.

Like King Tut in the story, mutts can look very different from other dogs. They can even be kind of weird! Most dogs of the same breed look a lot alike, so a purebred dog looks just like its mother or father. But mutts are definitely different! Because these dogs are a mix of different breeds, sizes, and shapes, mutts are unique! It's hard to find two mutts that look exactly alike.

Just like mutts are a mix of different physical traits, like color or size, they are a mix of different personalities and skills too. Many people believe that mutts are smarter and easier to train than purebred dogs. That's because these dogs can have the best parts of all the breeds that make them up. Mutts are often more healthy than purebred dogs, too. Because they are a mix of physical traits, they can keep the best of each breed that went into creating this unique kind of dog.

Mutts are more common than you might think. About three-quarters of all the dogs in animal shelters are mixed breeds. Many dogs that look like purebreds often have other breeds mixed in. Sometimes it's easy to tell what breeds make up a mutt. Other times the dog's background is a complete mystery, as it is with King Tut.

No matter what breeds make up their background, most mutts make wonderful pets and companions. It can be easier for mutts to get used to living in a home or being in different situations than a breed that is bred for a specific job, such as herding or hunting.

If you think about it, a lot of people are "mutts." We come from many different backgrounds and cultures. Mixed-breed dogs are just as good, if not better, than many purebred dogs. No matter how weird a dog looks or what its background is, mutts are tops when it comes to a canine companion.

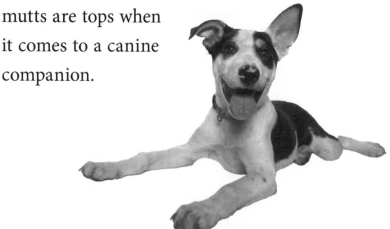

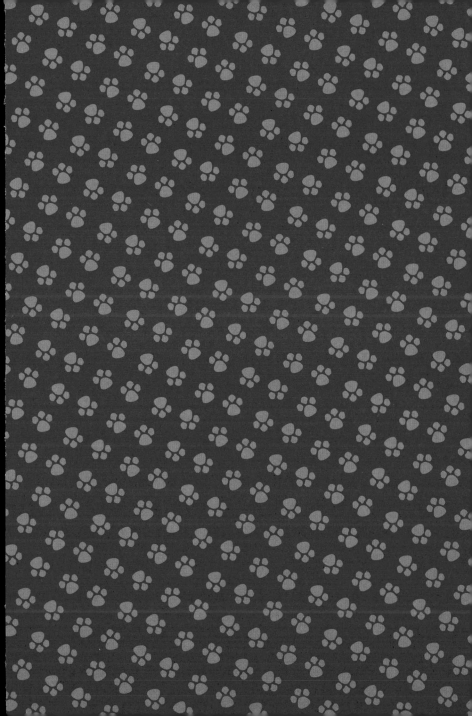

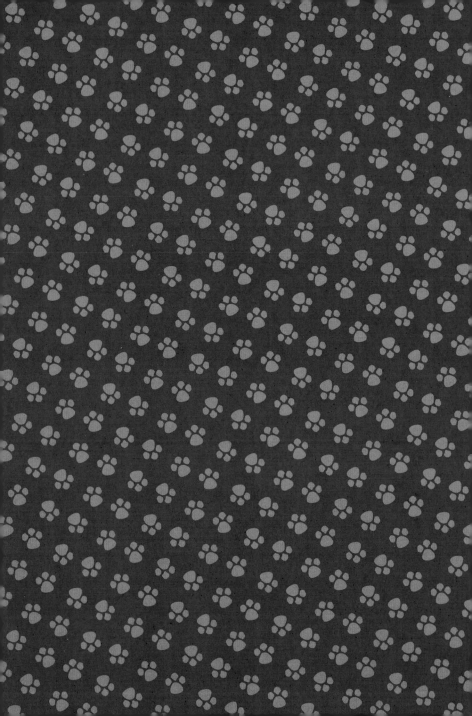